To Claire, Elliott, and Jack
K. G.

To the Sullivans
N. S.

Dorling Kindersley Publishing, Inc.
95 Madison Avenue
New York, New York 10016

Visit us on the World Wide Web at http://www.dk.com

Dorling Kindersley Publishing offers special discounts for bulk purchases for sales promotions or premiums.
Specific, large quantity needs can be met with special editions, including personalized covers,
excerpts of existing guides, and corporate imprints. For more information, contact Special Markets Dept.,
Dorling Kindersley Publishing, Inc., 95 Madison Ave., New York, NY 10016. Fax: 800-600-9098.

ISBN: 0-7894-2667-6

First published in Great Britain in 2000 by The Bodley Head Children's Books,
Random House, 20 Vauxhall Bridge Road, London SW1V 2SA

The text of this book is set in 23 point Lemonade Bold
Printed and bound in Singapore.

First American Edition, 2000
2 4 6 8 10 9 7 5 3 1

JP
GRAY
[28] p. col. ill.

Eat Your Peas

by Kes Gray   illustrated by Nick Sharratt

DORLING KINDERSLEY PUBLISHING, INC.

It was dinnertime again and Daisy knew just what her mom was going to say, before she even said it. "Eat your peas," said Mom.

Daisy looked down at the little green balls
that were ganging up on her plate.
"I don't like peas," said Daisy.

Mom sighed one of her usual sighs.
"If you eat your peas, you can
have a dish of ice cream," said Mom.

"I don't like peas," said Daisy.

"If you eat your peas, you can have a dish of ice cream and you can stay up an extra half hour."

"I don't like peas," said Daisy.

"If you eat your peas, you can have a dish of ice cream, stay up an extra half hour, and you can skip your bath."

"I don't like peas," said Daisy.

"If you eat your peas, you can have ten dishes of ice cream,

 stay up really late, you don't have to wash for

two whole months, and I'll buy

you a new bike."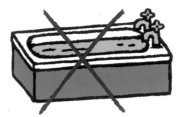

"I don't like peas," said Daisy.

"If you eat your peas, you can have 48 dishes of ice cream, stay up past midnight, you never have to wash again, I'll buy you two new bikes, and a baby elephant."

"I don't like peas," said Daisy.

"If you eat your peas, you can have 100 dishes of ice cream,

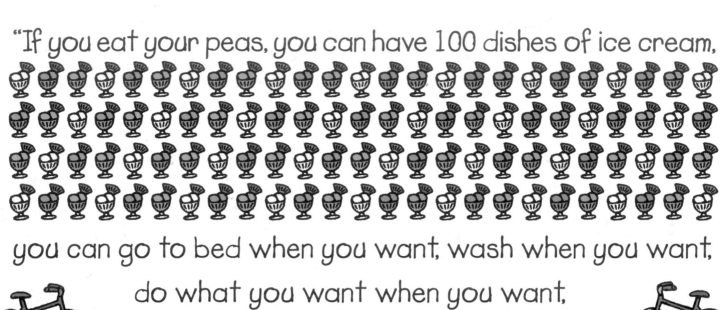

you can go to bed when you want, wash when you want,

do what you want when you want,

I'll buy you ten new bikes,

two pet elephants,   three zebras,   a penguin,

and a chocolate factory."

"I don't like peas," said Daisy.

"If you eat your peas, I'll buy you a supermarket packed full of ice cream,

you never have to go to bed again ever, or school

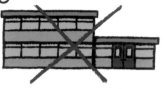 again, you never have to wash,

or brush your hair,

or shine your shoes,

or clean your bedroom,

I'll buy you a bike shop, a zoo, ten chocolate factories,

 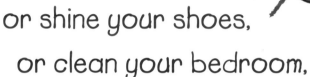 

I'll take you to Superland
for a week, and you can have your very

own space rocket with

double retro laser

blammers."

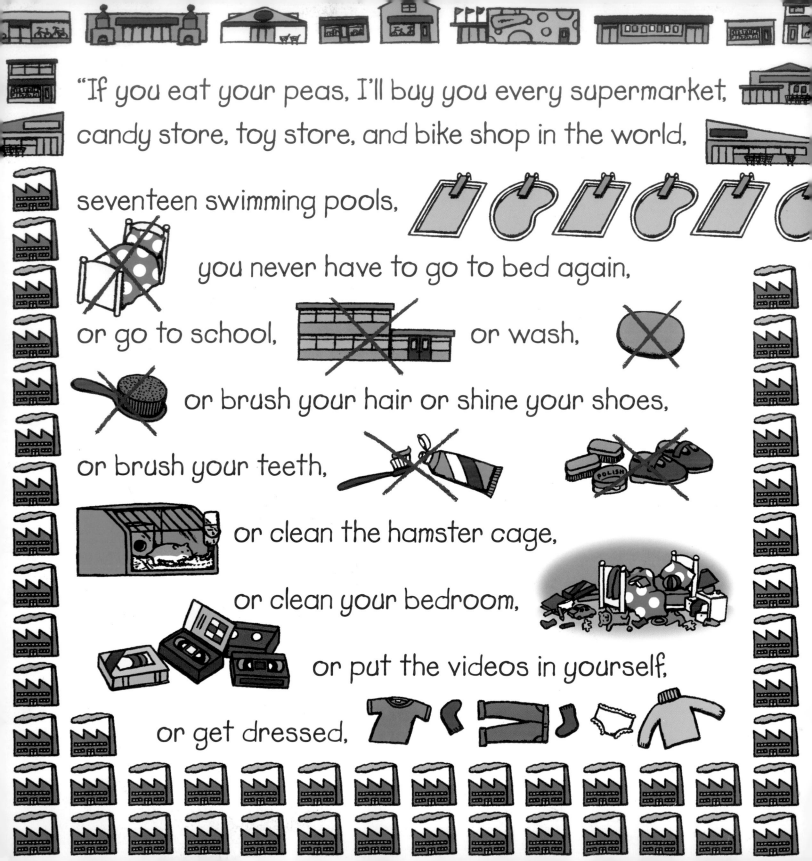

"If you eat your peas, I'll buy you every supermarket, candy store, toy store, and bike shop in the world,

seventeen swimming pools,

you never have to go to bed again,

or go to school, or wash,

or brush your hair or shine your shoes,

or brush your teeth,

or clean the hamster cage,

or clean your bedroom,

or put the videos in yourself,

or get dressed,

I'll buy you Africa

and ninety-two chocolate factories,

we'll move to Superland,

you can have all the space rockets you want,

I'll buy you the earth, the moon,

the stars, the sun,

and...and...and...

...and a new fluffy pencil case!"

"You really want me to eat my peas, don't you?" said Daisy.
"Yes," said Mom.

"OK, I'll eat my peas if you eat your brussels sprouts," said Daisy.

Mom looked down at her own plate
and her bottom lip began to quiver.
"But I don't like brussels sprouts," said Mom.

"Exactly!" said Daisy.
"You don't like
brussels sprouts and
I DON'T LIKE PEAS!"

But we both like ice cream!